Arabian Wisdom: Selections and Translations from the Arabic

by John Wortabet

Copyright © 11/11/2015
Jefferson Publication

ISBN-13: 978-1519251268

Printed in the United States of America

Table of Contents

INTRODUCTION

The wise sayings and proverbs of ancient and modern times, and in all the languages I know or to which I had access in translations, have always had a great attraction for me. Drawn from the experiences and study of human life, they have been reduced by wise men to short, pithy sentences, generally expressed in some quaint or striking form, for conveying sound moral truths. They are intended to be maxims of life, or rules of conduct, chiefly for the young, but may be read with pleasure and profit by both young and old. It was with such an object in view that the Editors of the *Wisdom of the East* series have lately issued a number of small books on this subject carefully translated by competent specialists, and which have been highly appreciated by the English press and public. Their chief desire, however, appears to be "that these books shall be the ambassadors of good-will and understanding between East and West," and also that "the great ideals and lofty philosophy of Oriental thought may help to a revival of that true spirit of Charity which neither despises nor fears the nations of another creed and colour." (See Editorial Note.)

It was also from such motives, but long before I had seen these books, that I have employed a part of my leisure hours in translating into Arabic some of the best sayings of M. Aurelius, Shakespeare, Tennyson, English and other proverbs, and, quite lately, selections from *The Instruction of Ptah-Hotep* and *Sadi's Scroll of Wisdom*. They were published in the best Arabic magazines, and have been read by many Christians, Moslems, and Jews in Egypt, Syria, and other countries; and I have been told by some of these Oriental readers that they found in them much matter for thought and instruction, while their views of the community and bonds of human nature among all nations, and in all parts of the world, have been broadened and enlarged.

The Arabic language is particularly rich in this kind of literature, and its proverbs are often appropriately introduced in conversation, letters, and books, and add much force to what is said or written. Many are light and colloquial, and bring a smile or laughter to both speaker and hearer; but many also are distinguished by their classical form and the serious weighty ideas which they convey or inculcate. It was easy, therefore, to find abundant material for this little book, but it was somewhat difficult to make a wise selection, to classify the different subjects under proper heads, and to translate Arabic idioms into good English. Other difficulties were when the proverb in Arabic is formed of two parts which assonate or rhyme, when the piquancy of a short sentence depends so much on the quaintness of its expression, when an untranslatable pun or play upon words is used, or when the phrase is too elliptical or too Oriental in its reference to be easily understood by English readers. The translation I have made is generally literal, sometimes free, but always true to the original. Some I have left in their Oriental form to show the Arabian bent of thought and mode of life. The renderings from the Koran are all mine, and I alone am responsible for them. All that I have tried to do was for ordinary readers—and for them alone.

5

Many proverbs are common to all languages, and in them all—notably among Semitic nations—there is often an exaggeration,[1] or a one-sided view,[2] or a paradox,[3] which must be taken with some latitude and with the natural limitations required by common sense. It will also be observed that many Arabic proverbs have a close resemblance to the Proverbs of Solomon, and often assume that rhetorical form or parallelism in which Hebrew poetry abounds when the same idea is repeated in other words, or where its positive and negative sides are put into contrast. The following quotation, taken from the eighth chapter of that book, may serve as an example of what has just been said, and as an appropriate introduction to this little book:

"Doth not wisdom cry,
And understanding put forth her voice?
Unto you, O men, I call;
And my voice is to the sons of men.
For my mouth shall utter truth;
And wickedness is an abomination to my lips.
For whoso findeth me findeth life,
And shall obtain favour of the Lord.
But he that sinneth against me wrongeth his own soul:
All they that hate me love death."

[1] "A fool throws a stone into a well, and a thousand wise men cannot get it out."

[2] "A man is safe when alone." "Paradise without human companions is not worth living in."

[3] "Do no good, and you will meet with no evil."

THE FIRST CHAPTER OF THE KORAN

In the name of God, who is abundant in mercy and compassion! Praise be to God, the Lord of the universe, the most merciful and compassionate, the Sovereign of the day of judgment. Thee alone we worship, and from Thee alone we seek help. Guide us to the right path—the path of them to whom Thou hast been gracious—not of them with whom Thou art angry, nor of them who have gone astray. Amen.[1]

[1] This opening chapter of the Koran—very short as it is—contains the fundamental principles of the whole book—the doctrine of God, His infinite mercy, the immortality of the soul, the rewards and punishments of the world to come, and the duty of prayer, and thanksgiving, and adoration, and obedience. It is a fair specimen of all that is best in the "Revealed Book" of the Moslems, and is as frequently repeated by them as the Lord's Prayer is by Christians.

REPENTANCE, AND GOD'S FORGIVING MERCY

Koran. O ye who believe, repent unto God, for He loveth them who are penitent. O ye who believe in me, who by much sin have done a great wrong to themselves, despair not of the mercy of God, for He forgiveth all sins. Verily He forgiveth and is merciful.

Traditions. Sorrow for sin is repentance. He who repents is like him who has not sinned.

Wise Sayings and Proverbs. No intercession succeeds so effectually as repentance.

The most truthful man is he who is true to his repentance.

Two sins only God does not forgive—worship of false gods and injury to men.

A SINNER'S CRY UNTO GOD[2]

[2] The original Arabic is in verse.

O Thou who knowest every thought, and hearest every cry,
Who art the source of all that is, or ever shall be,
Who art the only hope in every trouble,
The only help in every plaint and every woe,
Whose treasures of bounty and word creative are one,
God of all good, hear my prayer!

One sole plea I have—my need of Thee;
But needing Thee my need is filled.
One only resource I have—to stand and knock;
And if unheard at Thy mercy-gate, to whom shall I go?

Whom shall I call, what Name shall I invoke,
If Thy needy servant shall in vain Thy bounty seek?
But far be it from Thee, God of grace, to refuse a sinner's cry.
Too good and gracious art Thou to send me thus away.

Contrite, I stand at Thy door,
Believing that contrite prayer availeth much with Thee.
Suppliant, I stretch forth my hands,
And with all my soul look up to Thee.
Save me, God, from every ill, and be Thy favour ever mine!

FORGIVING OTHERS

Koran. God forgiveth past sins; let men forgive and pardon.
Forgive freely. Forgiving others is the nearest thing to piety.

Traditions. He who forgiveth others, God forgiveth him.

Be merciful, and you will have mercy; forgive and you will be forgiven.

Sayings and Proverbs. Of all things God loveth best forgiveness when one is able to inflict harm, and forbearance when one is angry.

The pleasure of forgiving is sweeter than the pleasure of revenge.

Forgiveness is perfect when the sin is not remembered.

The most wicked of men is he who accepts no apology, covers no sin, and forgives no fault.

Small men transgress, great men forgive.

A noble man condones and pardons, and when by chance he finds out a sin, he conceals it.

A man said to another who had spoken evil of him: "If what you have said be true, may God forgive me; and if false, may He forgive you."

CLEMENCY, FORBEARANCE, AND GENTLENESS

Koran. Those who worship the Merciful One are they who walk on the earth gently, and who, when fools speak to them, say "Peace." (25, 64.)

Traditions. Be friendly to him who would be unfriendly to you, give him who will not give you, and forbear with him who would do you harm.

Next to faith in God, the chief duty of man is to treat his fellow men with gentleness and courtesy.

Sayings and Proverbs. Gentleness is one of the noblest traits in a man's character.

A gentle man is a man of great beauty.

One of the surest evidences of gentleness is tenderness to fools.

The fierce anger of a foolish man is checked by gentleness as a fierce fire is extinguished by water.

Gentleness is sometimes an humiliation, and he who is always forbearing and patient may be trodden down by fools.

If you honour a vile man, you disgrace the code of honour.

HUMILITY

Humility is that line of conduct which is a mean between overbearing pride on the one hand and abject servility on the other, as economy is the middle term between extravagance and avarice.

Humility is the crown of nobility, a ladder to honour, and a means of procuring love and esteem.

He who humbleth himself, God lifteth him up.

When Abu-Bekr, "the righteous" (the first Khalif), was praised, he used to say: "O God, Thou knowest me better than I know myself, and I know myself better than they know me. Make me, I pray Thee, better than they suppose; forgive me what they know not, and lay not to my account what they say."

A wise man was once asked whether he knew of any good which is not coveted, or any evil which deserves no mercy, and he said: "Yes, they are humility and pride."

To despise a proud man is true humility.

TRUE NOBILITY

True nobility lies in high character and refined manners, not in noble birth or ancient pedigree.

A noble man is he who aims at noble ends—not he who glories in an ancestry mouldering in the dust.

A noble man is noble though he come to want, and a base man is base though he walks on pearls.

A lion is a lion though his claws be clipped, and a dog is a dog though he wear a collar of gold.

He who disregards his own honour gets no good from an honourable lineage.

Learning and high principles take the place of noble birth, and cover the shame of a low origin.

A branch tells of what stock it comes.

SELF-RESPECT, AND THE SENSE OF SHAME

Son of man, if you have no self-respect, do what you will.

Men see no fault in one who respects himself.

If you fear not the consequences of an evil life, and have no sense of shame, you are free to do what you will.

No, by God, life has no worth, and this world has no happiness to a man who has lost his self-respect and abandons himself to shamelessness.

There is no good in a man who is not ashamed of men.

He who has a brazen face has a craven heart.

To be ashamed before God is to obey His commandments and to avoid what He has forbidden; to be ashamed before men is to avoid all harm to them; and to be ashamed before one's self is to be chaste and clean when one is alone.

Be ashamed in your own sight more than in the sight of men.

He who does a thing in secret of which he would be ashamed if done openly, has no respect for himself.

He who respects not himself can have no respect for others.

I shall not kiss a hand which deserves to be cut off.

CHARACTER

A man is truly religious when he is truly good.

A good character is a great boon.

Kind words are the bonds of love.

A kind word is like an act of charity.

If you cannot help men with money, help them with a cheerful face and a kindly bearing.

No man is entitled to consideration unless he has these three things, or at least one of them: the fear of God to restrain him from evil, forbearance with wicked men, and a good nature towards all.

There are cases where not kindness but severity is necessary.

Kindness increases the love of friends, and diminishes the hatred of enemies.

Be firm after you have been kind.

God loves the man who is tender-hearted.

An evil nature is a calamity from which there is no escape.

If you hear that a mountain has moved from its place believe it, but if you hear that a man has changed his character do not believe it, for he will act only according to his nature.

An inherited quality may be traced back to the seventh grandfather.

There are four points in a good character from which all other good traits take their origin—prudence, courage, continence, and justice.

When a woman has had more than one husband in this life, she will, in the future state, be free to be the wife of him whose character she esteemed the most.

BENEVOLENCE

Koran. Do good unto others as God has done unto you.

Is the reward of kindness anything but kindness?

He who does a kindly act shall be recompensed tenfold.

Ye can never be righteous unless ye give away from that which ye love.

Traditions. The upper hand [which giveth] is better than the lower hand [which taketh].

God's creatures are the objects of His care, and He loveth best that man who is most helpful to them.

Proverbs. Do not be ashamed to give little, for it is less than that, if you give nothing.

If you give, give freely, and if you strike, strike boldly.

He who soweth kindness shall reap thanks.

What a man does for God is never lost.

Be merciful to him who is beneath you, and you will have mercy from Him who is above you.

The best kind of good is that which is done most speedily.

Inopportune kindness is injustice.

No true joy but in doing good and no true sorrow but in doing evil.

Cruelty to animals is forbidden by God.

A peacemaker gets two-thirds of the blows.

GENEROSITY

Generosity is to do a kindness before it is asked, and to pity and give a man who asks.

A generous man is nigh unto God, nigh unto men, nigh unto paradise, far from hell.

Overlook the faults of a generous man, for God helps him when he falls and gives him when he is needy.

A man who doeth good does not fall, and if he fall he will find a support.

Be not ashamed to give little—to refuse is less.

GRATITUDE

He is unthankful to God who is unthankful to man.

He who is unthankful for little is unthankful for much.

God continues His favours to him who is grateful.

He who is ungrateful for the good he receives deserves that it should be withdrawn from him.

Man can be thankful to God only so far as he does good to his fellow men.

If a man professes to thank God and his wealth decreases, his thanksgiving must be vitiated by his neglect of the hungry and naked.

Be grateful to him who has done you good, and do good to him who is grateful to you.

Gratitude takes three forms—a feeling in the heart, an expression in words, and a giving in return.

The most worthless things on earth are these four—rain on a barren soil, a lamp in sunshine, a beautiful woman given in marriage to a blind man, and a good deed to one who is ungrateful.

RECOMPENSE

To recompense good for good is a duty.

Neglect of recompense is contemptible.

If a man do you a favour recompense him, and if you are unable to do so, pray for him.

The worst kind of recompense is to requite evil for good.

Reproach faults by kindness, and requite evil by good.

There is no glory in revenge.

Meet insult by insult, and honour by honour. Evil can be repelled only by evil.

What you put into the pot you will take out in the ladle.

He who plays with a cat must bear its scratches.

He who lives in a house of glass should not throw stones at people.

Sins may lurk, but God deals heavy blows.

FLAUNTING KINDNESS

To carry a heavy rock to the summit of a mountain is easier than to receive a kindness which is flaunted.

The bane of a generous action is to mention it.

It is better to refuse a kindness than to be reminded of it.

I would not accept the whole world if I were to suffer the humiliation of being constantly reminded of the gift.

To bestow and flaunt a kindness, and to be stingy and refuse to do an act of kindness, are equally bad.

When you do a kindness hide it, and when a kindness is done to you proclaim it.

Do good, and throw it into the sea.

KNOWLEDGE

Koran. O God, increase my knowledge. Are they who know and they who know not equal?

He who has been given wisdom has been given a great good.

What ye have been given of knowledge is only a small part.

Above a learned man there is one more learned.

Traditions. Learned men are trustees to whom God has confided mankind.

Stars are the beauty of the heavens, and learned men are the ornament of a people.

Angels bend down their wings to a seeker of knowledge.

Proverbs. The rank of the learned is the highest of all ranks.

If learning does not give wealth it will give esteem.

Knowledge increaseth the honour of a nobleman, and bringeth men of low degree into the houses of kings.

A seat of learning is a garden of heaven.

Forgetfulness is the bane of knowledge.

It is difficult for a man to know himself.

Knowledge is a lamp from which men light their candles.

A mind without education is like a brave man without arms.

Kings govern men, and learned men govern kings.

That day in which I have learned nothing, and in which I have added nothing to my knowledge, is no part of my life.

He who seeks learning without study will attain his end when the raven becomes grey with age.

To every noble horse a stumble, and to every learned man an error.

Knowledge does not save from error, nor wealth from trouble.

The owner of the house knows best what is in it.

SPECULATIVE STUDIES

All speculative research ends in perplexing uncertainty.

I sought in the great sea of theoretical learning a bottom on which to stand—and found nothing but one wave dashing me against another.

After a lifetime of research and learning, I amassed nothing but such phrases as: "It is said," or "They say."

O erring reason, I am sick of thee! I take a single step and thou movest a whole mile away from me.

The object sought in abstruse study is either a truth which cannot be known, or a vain thing which it is useless to know.

THOUGHTS, DOUBTS

Most thoughts are wishes.

The thoughts of the wise are more trustworthy than the convictions of fools.

Do not confuse opinions with certainties.

If you are doubtful of a thing let it alone.

Remove doubts by enquiry.

A thing that is heard is not like a thing that is seen.

Do not believe all that you hear.

It is not wise to be sure of a thing only because you think so.

Where there is much difference of opinion it is difficult to know the truth.

To think well of others is a religious duty.

He who thinks well of others is a happy man.

He who has an evil thing in him thinks all men are like him.

If a man think well of you, make his thought true.

A poet says: "It was my habit to think well of others until experience taught me otherwise."

Be well with God and fear nothing.

Most men think well of themselves, and this is self-delusion.

WISDOM, PRUDENCE, EXPERIENCE

Reason is a light in the heart which distinguishes between truth and error.

A wise man sees with his heart what a fool does not see with his eyes.

Men should be judged according to their lights (reason).

A wise man is not he who considers how he may get out of an evil, but he who sees that he does not fall into it.

Actions are judged by their endings. If you desire a thing, consider its end.

A man cannot be wise without experience.

No wise man will be bitten twice from the same den.

No boon is so remunerative as reason.

Long experience is an addition to mind.

Consideration may take the place of experience.

A wise man is he who has been taught by experience.

One word is sufficient to the wise man.

A cheap offer makes a wise purchaser wary.

He who considers consequences will attain his object, and he who does not carefully think on them, evil will be sure to overtake him.

Everything has need of reason, and reason has need of experience.

Mind and experience are like water and earth co-operating— neither of which alone can bring forth a flower.

Reason and anxious thought are inseparable.

A wise man is never happy. (For in much wisdom is much grief, and he that increaseth knowledge increaseth sorrow.—ECCLES. i. 18.)

IGNORANCE, FOLLY

Ignorance is the greatest poverty.

Ignorance is death in life.

There is no evil so great as ignorance.

Folly is an incurable disease.

A foolish man is like an old garment, which if you patch it in one place becomes rent in many other places.

It is just as allowable to blame a blind man for want of sight as to blame a fool for his folly.

To bear the folly of a fool is indeed a great hardship.

The best way to treat a fool is to shun him.

The fool is an enemy to himself—how can he then be a friend to others?

An ignorant man is highly favoured, for he casts away the burden of life, and does not vex his soul with thoughts of time and eternity.

The most effectual preacher to a man is himself. A man never turns away from his passions unless the rebuke comes from himself to himself.

CONSULTATION

If you consult a wise man, his wisdom becomes yours.

Confide your secret to one only, and hear the counsel of a thousand. (In the multitude of counsellors there is safety. PROV. xi. 14.)

A counsellor is a trusted man.

When men consult together, they are led by the wisest among them.

The knowledge of two is better than the knowledge of one. Two heads are better than one.

Let your counsellor be one who fears God.

Consult a man of experience, for he gives you what has cost him much, and for which you give nothing.

A man who is older than yourself by a day is more experienced than you by a year.

Consult an older man and a younger, then decide for yourself.

The wisest may need the advice of others.

He who is wise, and consults others, is a whole man; he who has a wise opinion of his own, and seeks no counsel from others, is half a man; and he who has no opinion of his own, and seeks no advice, is no man at all.

No man can be sorry for seeking advice, or happy if he blindly follows out his own thoughts.

SPEAKING, WRITING, BOOKS

If it were not for the faculty of speech, man would be nothing more than a silent picture or a contemptible animal.

The tongue is the best part of man.

Man is hidden behind his tongue.

A man's talk shows what kind of mind he has.

What you write is the truest thing that can be said of you.

The words of eloquent men are like a mighty army, and their writings like glittering swords.

Note down in writing what you learn. All knowledge which is not committed to writing is lost.

The best handwriting is that which is most easily read.

A bad pen is like an unruly, undutiful child.

If you value a book you will read it through.

If you write a book, be ready to encounter criticism.

A book is like a garden carried in the pocket.

A book is an eloquent, silent companion, or a speaking friend answering and questioning you.

Books are the food of minds.

There is something wise in every proverb.

The tongues of men are the pens of truth.

Poets, love-stricken, ramble up and down in every valley.

Poetry is one of the musical instruments of Satan.

SILENCE, GUARDED SPEECH

Wise men are silent.

Silence is often more eloquent than words.

Be not hasty with your tongue. If words are silver, silence is gold.

Not all that is known should be said.

Silence is a wise thing, but they who observe it are few.

When the mind becomes large speech becomes little.

Restrain your tongue from saying anything but what is good.

An unguarded word may do you great harm.

A man who talks much is open to much blame.

The most faulty of men are they that are most loquacious in matters which do not concern them.

To guard his tongue is one of the best traits in a man's character.

Man is saved from much evil if he guard his tongue.

The tongue is a lion which must be chained, and a sharp sword which must be sheathed.

Nothing on earth is so deserving of a long imprisonment as the tongue.

Beware of saying anything of which you may be ashamed.

It is better to regret a thing which you did not say than a thing which you did say.

A slip of the foot is safer than a slip of the tongue. A false step may break a bone which can be set, but a slip of the tongue cannot be undone.

A thrust of the tongue is sharper than the thrust of a lance.

A word may cause much trouble, destroy a home, or open a grave.

A great tree grows out of a small seed.

The difference between loquacity and silence is like the difference between the noisy frog and the silent whale.

Wisdom is made up of ten parts—nine of which are silence, and the tenth is brevity of language.

A man conceals his ignorance by his silence.

He who says what he should not say, will have to hear what he would not like to hear.

He who talks much does little.

What is said at night the day blots out.

TRUTHFULNESS

Koran. O ye that believe, fear God and be truthful! Verily God recompenseth the truthfulness of the truthful.

Traditions. Be ever truthful, for truthfulness leads to righteousness, and righteousness leads to heaven.

Veracity brings peace to the heart.

No man's religion can be right until his heart become right, nor can his heart become right until his tongue is right.

Keep to the truth though it may harm thee, and keep away from falsehood though it may profit thee.

A man can be perfect only when he speaks the truth and acts according to the truth.

Proverbs. Truth is the sword of God, which always cleaves when it smites.

Truth is armed with horns.

By truth man is saved from evil.

If falsehood saves from trouble truth saves much more.

When thou speakest be truthful, and when thou actest be gentle.

An ignorant man who is true is better than a clever man who is false.

There are two kinds of truthfulness, and the greatest of them is that which may do thee harm.

If truth and falsehood were pictured they would be represented by a terrible lion and a cunning fox.

It is better to die a truthful man than to live the life of a liar.

TRUTHFULNESS TO PROMISES

Koran. Be true to a covenant, for a covenant holds a man responsible. Be faithful to your pledged covenants and keep your oaths.

Traditions. A man who keeps not his word has no religion.

A true man's word is like an oath.

Be truthful in what you say, faithful to your promise, and careful of what is entrusted to you.

A pledged word is as if you had made the gift.

Proverbs. A true man keeps his promise.

A pledged word has the same value as a debt.

The promise of a true man is a greater obligation than a debt.

That man is a hypocrite who prays and fasts, but is untruthful in what he says, false to his word, and unfaithful in discharging a trust.

TRUTHFULNESS TO SECRETS

To keep a secret is a divine law.

A secret is a trust, and to betray it is perfidy.

The least of all noble traits is to keep a secret, and the greatest is to forget it.

He controls himself most who hides a secret from his friends.

When a secret is known to more than two, it becomes public.

He who seeks a place to hide his secret reveals it.

Walls have ears.

It is unwise to confide a secret to two tongues and four ears.

Your secret is your captive, betray it and you become its captive.

A man should be a tomb in which a secret is deposited.

If you keep your secret you are safe, and it will be to your sorrow if you reveal it.

Hearts are the depositaries of secrets, lips their locks, and tongues their keys.

The hearts of the wise are the fortresses of secrets.

DECEIT

Deceit does more harm to the deceitful than to the deceived.

If a man commit these three things they will rise against him in judgment and punishment—aggression, perfidy, and deceit.

To be true to the perfidious is perfidy, and to deceive the deceitful is lawful.

In deceiving your neighbour be more wary than when he is trying to deceive you.

When one would deceive you, and you feign to be deceived, you have deceived him.

He who would deceive one who cannot be deceived is only deceiving himself.

He who allows himself to be deceived by what his enemy says is the greatest enemy to himself.

A wise man neither deceives nor is deceived.

If a man believe in a stone it will do him good.

Self-deception is one of the forms of folly.

Most men think well of themselves, and this is self-delusion.

Vain desires are rarely realised, but they may give comfort in sorrow or pleasure in empty hope.

EXERTION, PERSEVERANCE, SUCCESS

A man obtains only what he strives for.

He who seeks and struggles shall find.

Struggles bring the most unlikely things within reach.

When a man makes up his mind to do a thing it becomes easy for him to do it.

If you have a clear thought, be decided, and hesitate not—if you decide, hesitate not, but carry it out speedily.

You must be ready to confront difficulties if you would realise your hopes.

It is the part of man to strive, and not to rely on the favours of Fortune.

Not every one who seeks shall find, nor every one who is indifferent be denied.

Beware of giving up hope in what you earnestly seek.

A wise man perseveres, and is not easily turned away.

Not by fitful efforts, but by constancy, is an end secured.

The most profitable labour is that which is most persevering— though it may not be strenuous.

A moderate success is better than overwhelming work.

Success comes to him who abjures procrastination.

The world is the booty of the skilful.

The most wonderful thing in the world is the success of a fool and the failure of a wise man.

A pleasing manner is a great aid to success.

It is the duty of man to do his utmost, but he is not responsible for success.

Do not undertake a work for which you are not competent.

What can a tirewoman do with an ugly face?

OPPORTUNITIES

Opportunities move like clouds, or pass rapidly like meteors.

Seize a thief before he seizes you.

Take advantage of the light of day before the night sets in.

Seize on opportunities, for they are either a spoil if improved, or a grief if neglected.

Good judgment means a seizure of opportunities.

Keep quiet until the occasion presents itself.

An action may be good if done at a fitting season, or evil if done at an improper time.

Procrastination means evil.

Put your bread into the oven while it is hot.

If you undertake a work do it speedily.

Profit by occasions when they turn up, and do not worry about an evil which has not yet come.

Time is a sharp sword—strike with it before you are struck by it.

If you have not sown, and see a reaper in the field, you will regret a lost opportunity.

ECONOMY

Economy saves half the cost of living.

The value of economy is equal to half of your profits.

Frugality saves a man from poverty.

Little with economy is better than much with waste.

Poverty with freedom from debt is great wealth.

If you count beforehand you will thrive.

The sea is made up of drops and the mountain of grains.

My son, take a middle course between stinginess and extravagance, parsimony and prodigality.

Extravagance dissipates great riches, and economy increases them when they are small.

Extravagance ever leads to misery and ruin.

Extravagance does as much harm to life as it adds to the pleasures of living.

In all things take a middle course.

Charity lies between two charities—one to yourself, the other to your needy fellow man.

If you are too soft you will be squeezed, and if you are too dry you will be broken.

He who spends and reckons not, ends in ruin and knows not.

He who buys cheap meat will regret his purchase when it is served up.

VICISSITUDES OF FORTUNE

Man is like an ear of wheat shaken by the wind—sometimes up and sometimes down.

Man is a target to the accidents of time.

One day for us, and one day against us.

With to-day there is to-morrow.

To every Moses there is a Pharaoh.

There is no day which has not its opposite.

The changes of fortune show what a man is made of.

There is no joy which is not followed by sorrow.

When Fortune brings a great good, she follows it by a great evil.

Fortune gives lavishly, and then turns round and takes away.

When a man has attained his highest hope, let him expect that its downfall is near by.

When a thing waxes to perfection it begins rapidly to wane.

When distress reaches its utmost, relief is close at hand.

What is past is dead.

Every ascent has a descent, and every trouble has an end.

Do not worry—between one twinkle of the eye and that which follows it things may change.

I have looked far and wide, and saw nothing on the faces of men but looks of perplexity or regret.

To complain of one's grief, except to God, is an humiliation.

He who thinks that Fortune will always favour him is a fool.

Follow the tracks of the fortunate man and you will come to fortune.

PATIENCE

God is with them that are patient. God loveth them that are patient (*Koran*).

Patience is one-half of religious duty.

There are two kinds of patience—one is for something which you desire, the other in something which you hate; and he is a strong man who can combine them both.

Patience is mostly needed at the first shock.

Grief is dispelled by patience.

The device of a man who hath no device is patience.

So long as there is a claimant, no just case is ever lost.

Patience is a bitter cup, which the strong alone can drink.

A misfortune is one, but it becomes two to the impatient.

Patience is one of the gifts of heaven.

He who is impatient to hear one word will have to listen to many words.

Difficulties can be overcome only by patience.

It is a good omen when your messenger is delayed.

Rarely does a patient man fail in obtaining that which he seeks.

Be patient—every cloud dissipates, and every evil which does not continue is a small thing.

He who receives the strokes is not like him who counts them.

CONTENTMENT

Contentment is to refrain from coveting what others have.

Contentment is a treasure which is inexhaustible.

The most thankful of men is he who is contented.

He who seeks riches must seek them in contentment.

Give freely, and be content with little.

A contented man is happy in life.

Life is a vanishing space of time, and he alone vanquishes its changing fortunes who lives in contentment.

Be content with what God has given you, and you will be the richest of men.

If you cannot have what you want, be content with what you have.

If all cannot be obtained, a part may be attained.

There is relief in despair.

CHEERFULNESS

God loves a cheerful man.

A main part of friendship is cheerfulness.

Cheerfulness denotes a generous nature, as a flower denotes fruit.

The first duty of a host is cheerfulness.

He who is sparing in cheerfulness is more sparing in doing a kindness.

A cheerful countenance is a presage of good.

A bright face and bright eyes are a greater boon than a rich inheritance.

The expression of the eyes shows what is in the heart.

An expression of the face may be more eloquent than that of the tongue.

The face of an enemy betrays his secret thoughts.

No one has ever harboured a secret which may not be discovered by a slip of the tongue or an expression of the face.

Hope for good from one who has a beautiful face.

A gloomy look is an omen of ill, and a bright face is good news.

Life has no cloud to an ignorant man, to one who heeds not past or future events, and to him who deceives himself and constrains his soul to seek and hope for what is impossible.

WAR

War is an evil thing to both victor and vanquished.

It is better to avoid than to make war.

The most honourable death is on the battlefield.

To die in battle from a thousand cuts of the sword is easier than to die in bed.

He who incites soldiers to courage in action is of more value than a thousand fighting men.

An army to a king is like wings to a bird.

To carry out a well-devised plan in war is more effectual than strokes and thrusts.

A battle is fought by feints and stratagems.

What an easy thing is a battle to one who looks on at a distance!

Patient constancy is the key to victory.

Two wolves kill a lion. Two weak men vanquish one that is strong.

Beware of aggression in war—for it can lead to no glory in victory.

To overcome the weak has all the shame of a defeat.

A butcher is not frightened at the sight of a multitude of sheep.

To retire from an unsuccessful battle is defeat.

Magnanimity to captives, and mercy to the fallen, are a hymn of praise to God for victory.

ANGER

The first part of anger is madness and the second is regret.

Passion and blindness are inseparable mates.

Beware of anger, for it ends in the humiliation of apology.

Anger leads to all kinds of evil.

When you are angry be silent.

It is not a trait of noble character to be hasty either in anger or in revenge.

The anger of a fool reveals itself in what he says, and the anger of a wise man in what he does.

Quarrelsomeness is a contemptible habit.

Call not yourself a man so long as you are angry.

HATRED, MALICE

Of all men God abhors most an implacable enemy.

Of all things nothing is so bad as the making of enemies.

Of all evils nothing is so hard to be borne as the triumph of an enemy.

Rejoice not over a fallen man—he may rise and you may fall.

Despise no enemy, however insignificant he may be—see how the shadow of the earth causes an eclipse of the moon, or how a midge brings a tear to the eye of a lion.

He who makes enemies shall have many a restless night.

He who has many enemies, let him expect a downfall.

When anger is repressed by reason of inability to do immediate harm, it retires into the heart in the form of malice and breeds these vices—envy, triumph over the enemy's ill, repulsion of friendly approaches, contempt, slander, derision, personal violence, and injustice.

MURDER

The first thing which shall be taken up in the Day of Judgment is murder.

Man is a building made by God, and he who destroys the building of God shall be demolished.

Put no man to undeserved death, for God forbids murder.

Announce violent death to the murderer, and poverty to the adulterer, though after a season.

ENVY

The difference between envy and emulation is, that in the first the desire is for the cessation of a good enjoyed by another, and in the second the desire is for the possession of a similar good.

An envious man is angry with God for His favours to other men.

Every favoured man is envied.

A lordly man is always an object of admiration or of envy.

Beware of envy, for it shows itself in you, not in him whom you envy.

Envy is a disease for which there is no cure.

Envy is a disease which does more harm to the envious than to the envied.

All enmity may be overcome except that which comes from envy.

There can be no peace in the heart of an envious man.

A man cannot be happy if he be malicious, envious, or ill-tempered.

Keep your affairs to yourself, for every favoured man is an object of envy.

Envy may be cured only by a sure knowledge that it is a cause of much pain to you and no evil to him whom you envy—so you must shun it if you would not be an enemy to yourself and a friend to your enemy.

Envy consumes man, as rust corrodes iron.

He who strains his neck to look at one above him gets nothing but pain.

Envy no man except him who is good.

RASHNESS

Beware of rashness, for it has well been called the Mother of Regrets.

He who acts hastily either makes a blunder, or comes very near it.

He who is deliberate is either right, or very nearly so.

A hasty act comes from the Evil One, and a deliberate act from God.

Haste is the resort of the weak.

LAZINESS

Hopes are never realised by sloth.

A lazy man can never succeed in life.

41

It is one of the signs of weakness to leave things to fate.

A lazy man loses what is due to him.

Weakness and sloth lead to ruin.

A man gets tired of having nothing to do, as he gets tired of work.

If work is hard, want of work is a great evil.

Youth, riches, and leisure are the great corrupters of life.

The head of an idle man is the workshop of Satan.

AVARICE, STINGINESS, GREED

Avarice and faith in God can never live together in the heart of man.

Avarice and ill-nature have no place in the heart of a good man.

Avarice is the parent of all evil dispositions.

The riches of an avaricious man go either to naught or to an heir.

He who is close-fisted shall be treated in a like manner.

A man who is miserly to himself cannot be generous to others.

An avaricious man is more lavish of his life than of his money.

A liberal man lives on his riches, a miser is eaten up by them.

A miser lives the life of a poor man in this world, and will be judged as a rich man in the world to come.

He who makes his morsel large will be choked.

Avarice is the murderer of the miser.

Greed is the mate of sorrow.

Strong wine is not more destructive to reason than greed.

An old man continues to be young in two things—love of money and love of life.

COMPLAINT, BLAME

To God alone I make my plaint of sorrow and grief (*Koran* 12, 86).

To bewail grief, except to God, is an humiliation.

Lamentation is the weapon of the weak.

A good man sees his own faults and is blind to the faults of others.

Censure your friend by kindness, and return the evil which he may have done to you by acts of favour.

To blame a friend is better than to lose him.

No man is free from faults.

If you count your friend's faults you will have no friend left.

An absent man has his apology with him.

He who compels you to blame him has made up his mind to forsake you.

43

Open blame is better than secret malice.

Blame not, nor boast, until a year and a half shall have passed away.

He who has a needle under his arm it will prick him.

There is no wood which has no smoke in it.

Among all snakes there is not one that is good.

You are your own enemy.

MARRIAGE

The advantages of marriage are purity of life, children, pleasures of home, and the happiness of exertion for the comfort of wife and children.

This life is a joy, and its greatest delight is a good wife.

An honourable marriage is a stepping-stone to honour.

Take a wife not for her beauty, but for her virtues.

Chastity united to beauty makes a wife perfect.

Three things contribute to long life—a large house, an obedient wife, and a swift horse.

The violence of love vanishes soon after marriage. If the love of bride and bridegroom were to endure, the Resurrection Day would be at hand.

A man has no portion in the love of women when he becomes grey, or when he loses his fortune.

The lover's eye is blind.

The disgrace of a woman is abiding.

Take the high-road, though it turn; and marry a woman of good birth, though she may have been passed by.

Women are the snares of Satan.

Happy is the woman who dies before her husband.

It is better to have a thousand enemies out of the house than one in it.

The girl who has many suitors, and makes no choice of one of them, is doomed to become an old maid.

CHILDREN

Children are a gift from God.

A child is a flower which has come down from Paradise.

Nothing is dearer than a child, except a grandchild.

When your son is young, train him; when he is grown, make a brother of him.

That child is loved most who is young until he is grown up, or sick until he recovers, or absent until he returns home.

Your riches and your children are a temptation to you (*Koran*).

Happy is the woman who has first daughters, then sons.

If you do not train up your child, time will do it.

The training of children is like chewing stones.

Your riches and children are your enemies—beware of them (*Koran*).

The joy of parents in their children prolongs life.

Sorrow for a child is a burning fire in the heart.

He who is not tender to his child shall find no tenderness in God to him.

Your children are not too many for Death, nor is your money too much for a rapacious governor.

FILIAL DUTY

When your father and mother become old, and you take them into your house, say not a word of impatience to them, nor rebuke them, but speak graciously, and be humble to them, and say: "O my God, be merciful to them, even as they tended me when I was young" (*Koran*).

Be dutiful to your father, and your son shall be dutiful to you.

He who is ill-mannered to his father will be ill-treated by his son.

The good-will of parents procures the good-will of God.

The central gate of heaven is open to the man who has been dutiful to his parents.

Paradise is open at the command of mothers.

You, and all that you have, belong to your father.

A daughter is always proud of her father.

An unmarried daughter has a broken wing.

BROTHERS, RELATIONS

A man who has no brother is like one who has a left arm and no right. A brother is a wing.

When evil befalls you, you will know the value of a brother.

Your brother is he who shares your distress.

The same regard is due to the eldest brother from the youngest as that which is due to a parent from his child.

God helps him who helps his brother. Who forsakes his brother will be forsaken by God.

A man is a mirror in which his brother's likeness is seen.

The best man among you is he who is best to his relations.

Blood does not become water.

Honour your tribe, for they are the wing with which you fly.

The measure of a man's greatness is that of his tribe (clan, party).

Be friendly to your relations, but do not depend on your relationship.

If it were not for my own arm, my mouth would have nothing to eat.

FRIENDS, COMPANIONS

A friend is a second self and a third eye.

A true man is he who remembers his friend when he is absent, when he is in distress, and when he dies.

A friend is known only in adversity.

If your friend is sweet, do not eat him up.

If you would keep a friend, do not lend him money nor borrow from him.

Keep to your old friends—your new friends will not be so constant.

You may find in a friend a brother who was not born of your mother.

The noblest man is he whose friendship may be easily obtained, and whose enmity can be incurred only with difficulty.

He is a weak man who can make no friends, and still weaker is he who loses them.

When my vine was laden with grapes, my friends were many; when the grapes were finished, my friends disappeared.

Friendship may come down by inheritance from ancestors, and so may hatred.

Nothing makes us feel so lonely as solitude, and nothing makes us so cheerful as freedom from evil companions.

Without human companions, Paradise itself would be an undesirable place to live in.

A man's character is judged by the character of his companions.

Smoke is no less an evidence of fire than that a man's character is that of the character of his associates.

He who associates with a suspected person will himself be suspected.

NEIGHBOURS

He is a good man who is a good neighbour.

No man enters heaven who is a bad neighbour.

A good neighbour is he who is not only harmless, but bears harm with patience.

Be friends, but do not become neighbours.

In social life be as friends, in business as strangers.

Prefer a near neighbour to a distant brother.

SALUTATION, VISITING

Return a salutation by something better, or at least by something as good (*Koran*).

A warm greeting renews friendship.

Respect is due to a visitor.

The best of men is a rich man who visits the poor, and the worst is a poor man who visits the rich.

Go a mile to see a sick man, go two miles to make peace between two men, and go three miles to call on a friend.

Make your visits short, especially to the sick.

To visit too often is tiresome to your friends, and to visit too rarely is less than what is due to friendship.

Your calls will be best appreciated when they are seasonable and not too frequent.

Too much familiarity is a cause of coolness among friends.

Do not associate much with men; if you do, shut your eyes to their faults, and bear consequent trouble.

LOVE OF COUNTRY AND HOME

Love of one's own country is a religious duty.

A true man yearns towards his native country, and longs for his home as a lion longs for his lair.

It is a sign of sound judgment when the heart craves for country and home.

He is better to suffer hardship in one's own country than to enjoy ease in a foreign land.

God blesses the land which is loved by its people.

As a nurse who has brought you up, has a special claim on you, so has your country.

He is an unwise man who alienates himself from his country and home.

If it were not for love of country, unhappy lands would be desolate.

It is an honour to you to love the land and house where you were born.

An old man is most comfortable in his own house.

TRAVELLING

In travelling you will find health and profit.

If water stagnates long it becomes foul.

A roaming dog is better than a couching lion.

During a journey a man's character is weighed and revealed.

The day on which a journey is begun is half the journey done.

HEALTH

Health is a crown on the head of the hale, invisible except to the sick.

Sound health is beyond all price.

The greatest gift to man is a long healthy life.

If there be anything more valuable than life, it is sound health.

It is wonderful that the envious see not the blessing of good health.

No man appreciates the worth of health until he is afflicted with disease.

If your dinner is light, your dreams will be pleasant.

So long as the head is free from trouble, the body will be sound.

YOUTH AND OLD AGE

An old man among his people is like a prophet sent from God.

To venerate old age is to revere God.

Youth is a kind of madness.

The wisest young men are they who follow the good example of the old, and the most foolish old men are they who follow the bad example of the young.

It is the duty of every one to be tender to the young and respectful to the old.

An old man should not give up his old habits, nor take to new ones.

An old man speaks of what he has seen, and a young man speaks of what he has heard.

Grey hairs are a sign of wisdom, and are beautified by reverence.

A hoary head is a rich cream churned by long years.

Grey hairs are a message from the other world.

After old age there is nothing but infirmity or death.

An old man cries out, "O that youth would return for a day, that I might relate to it what the roll of years has done to me!"

The hair often becomes white, not from the succession of years, but from a succession of evils.

Life is a parting shadow and youth a departing guest.

When a young man says he is hungry, believe him; but when he says he is tired, do not believe him.

DEATH

All life ends in death.

When I see all paths leading men unto death, and no paths leading from death unto us—no traveller there ever returning—not one of ages past ever remaining—I see that I also shall assuredly go where they have gone.

If death be surely inevitable, be not a fool and die a coward's death.

Death is a cup which every man must drink, and the grave a door which every man must enter.

If we are hastening to death, why all this impatience with the ills of life?

This life is a sleep, the life to come is a wakening; the intermediate step between them is death, and our life here is a disturbed dream.

He who dreads the causes of death, they will surely seize him— do what he will to evade them.

Death, so far as one can see, strikes at random, killing the man whom he hits, and leaving the man whom he misses to old age and decrepitude.

Death covers all faults.

APPENDIX

WHAT IS RIGHTEOUSNESS?

"Righteousness is not that ye turn your faces [in prayer] to the east or west; but righteousness is to him who believeth in God and the Last Day, and Angels, and Revealed Books, and Prophets; who giveth cheerfully from his substance to kinsmen, orphans, the needy, the wayfarer, and to them that ask; who freeth the prisoner and the slave; who offereth prayers at their appointed times, and giveth the ordained alms; to them who fulfil the covenants to which they have bound themselves, and who are patient in times of distress, and pain, and struggle: these are they who are sincere [in religion], and who fear to do evil (*Koran* 2, 172)."

This fine passage from the Koran is considered by Moslem commentators as the most comprehensive statement of the duties of man: "Sound faith, a good social life, and right culture of the soul" (El-Beidaway).

Instructions of Ali Ibn-abi Talib, the first Khalif to his son—"My son, fear God both secretly and openly; speak the truth, whether you be calm or angry; be economical, whether you be poor or rich; be just to friend and foe; be resigned alike in times of adversity and prosperity. My son, he who sees his own faults has no time to see the faults of others; he who is satisfied with the allotments of Providence does not regret the past; he who unsheaths the sword of aggression will be killed by it; he who digs a pit for his brother will fall into it; he who forgets his own sin makes much of the sin of another; he who takes to evil ways will be despised; he who commits excesses will be known to do them; he who associates with the base will be subject to constant suspicion; he who remembers death will be content with little in this world; he who boasts of his sins before men, God will bring him to shame."

THE EXPERIENCES OF AN OLD MAN

"I have heard many sermons and had many counsels, but I have heard no preacher so effective as my grey hairs, and no counsellor so effectual as the voice of my own conscience. I have eaten the most choice food, and drunk the best kinds of wine, and enjoyed the love of the most beautiful women; but I found no pleasure so great as that of sound health. I have swallowed the bitterest food and drink, but I found nothing so bitter as poverty. I have worked at iron and carried heavy weights, but I found no burden so heavy as that of debt. I have sought wealth in all its forms, but found no riches so great as those of contentment."

EIGHT MEN WHO DESERVE TO BE SLAPPED ON THE FACE

He who despises a man of power; he who enters a house uninvited and unwelcomed; he who gives orders in a house not his own; he who takes a seat above his position; he who speaks to one who does not listen to him; he who intrudes on the conversation of others; he who seeks favours from the ungenerous; and he who expects love from his enemies.

FORBEARANCE

The following story is related by Arabian authors of Ma'an Ibn-Zaidah, who, from a humble origin, rose to be Governor of Irak. The story is probably not altogether historical, but it shows the high ideal of Arab moralists as regards forbearance and gentleness.

An Arab of the desert, who had heard much of the great gentleness of Ibn-Zaidah, came one day to try him. Entering abruptly into his presence he addressed him thus (in verse):

"Rememberest thou when thy bed-covering was a sheepskin and thy sandals made of camel-skin?"

Ma'an answers (in prose): Yes, I remember, and I have not forgotten it.

The Arab. Praise be to God, who hath given thee a great rule, and taught thee how to sit on a throne!

Ma'an. Yes, praise to Him in every condition of life!

Arab. Never shall I greet Ma'an as an emir should be greeted!

Ma'an. Greeting is an ordinance among Arabs in which you are free to take what form you like.

Arab. An Emir who eats sweet pastry in secret, and entertains his guest with barley bread!

Ma'an. The food is our own: we eat what we like and give others what we like.

Arab. I shall leave a land in which thou dwellest, and depart, though the hand of Fortune is hard upon me.

Ma'an. Brother Arab, if thou stay, thou art welcome; and if thou depart, peace go with thee.

Arab. Son of shame, give me something for my journey, for I have decided to go.

Ma'an (*to his treasurer*): Give him a thousand pieces of money.

Arab. Noble prince, I have heard much of thy great forbearance, and came only to try thee. Thy gentleness is indeed very great, and has no like among men. I pray God that thy life may be long, and thy forbearance be ever a noble example to which men may look up!

TRUTHFULNESS TO TRUST

The following historical incident is related by Arab authors as the highest example of faithfulness to trust. Al-Samau'al (Samuel) was the emir of a Jewish tribe in Southern Arabia, shortly before the time of Mohammed. A friend of his, before setting out on a journey, left with him some very fine mailed armour. This friend was killed in a battle, and one of the kings of Syria demanded the arms. Al-Samau'al refused to give them up except to the rightful heir, and the king laid siege to him in one of his fortresses. One day his son fell into the hands of the enemy, and the king threatened to kill him if the arms were not given up. Again he refused, and from the turrets of the castle saw his son put to death. The siege was soon after raised, and the arms were delivered to the heirs of his friend.

TRUTHFULNESS TO PLEDGE

The terms of surrender at the capture of Jerusalem by Saladin, in 1187, were that the Crusaders should retire with their goods from that city to one of the garrisoned ports which were held by the Franks, on the payment of ten pieces of gold for each man. As they were filing out of the city, and handing in their ransom-money, Saladin and his generals looked on, watching the proceedings. The patriarch's turn came, and he was followed by a number of mules laden with much treasure. Saladin made no sign, but his generals said: "Sire, the conditions of surrender were for private property, not for such treasures of money, which we urgently need for carrying on the war." To this appeal he replied: "No, I have pledged my word, and for the ten pieces of gold agreed upon he shall be free."

But just as he was so strictly truthful to his word, he was equally severe in exacting the same truthfulness from his foes. Thus after the great battle of Hittin, when the Crusading army was utterly crushed, a large number of prisoners fell into his hands, including the King of Jerusalem and Count Raymond de Chatillon, Governor of Kerak, to the east of the Jordan. The count was a bad, dishonourable man, and had (not long before) shamelessly violated an armistice, and fallen on a defenceless Moslem caravan which was passing through his province, killing the men and seizing their property. When Saladin heard of this base breach of the laws of war he was furious, and vowed that if this perfidious prince should ever fall into his power, he would kill him with his own hand; and now the count was his prisoner. The day of battle, in the month of August, had been very hot, and the Crusaders, with their heavy coats of mail, and without a drop of water to drink, had suffered terribly from thirst. The tents of Saladin were pitched near the Lake of Tiberias, and when the king and the count were brought in, the king asked for a drink of water—which Saladin at once ordered. A large goblet of iced water was handed to him, and after quenching his thirst he passed the cup to the count. Saladin looked on, but said nothing until the count had finished drinking, and he then said to him: "I gave no orders for drink for you; if I had, your life would have been safe by our laws of hospitality. But you are a bad, faithless man, who broke the terms of our truce, and you shall now suffer the death which you deserve," and with one stroke of his scimitar he cut off his head. He then sent for the Knights of St. John, of whom there were about a thousand prisoners, and said to them: "So far as you have been brave warriors, and cost the Moslems many a man, I have nothing to say; but you have not been fair and honourable in our wars, nor true to your engagements, and I now offer you the option of Islam or death."

To a man they all chose death in preference to adopting a faith which they hated; and so they were led to the shores of the lake and there beheaded.

More than seven hundred years after these tragic events, William II., the present Emperor of Germany, who is a descendant of the Crusading Princes, and a Knight of the Brandenburg branch of the order of St. John, came to Damascus in 1898; and one of the first things he did there was to visit the tomb of Saladin, and lay on it a wreath of flowers. It was a generous and beautiful and well-deserved tribute to the memory of a truly great man, from whom the Christian nations of his times learned much of their chivalry and truthfulness to their pledged word.

A THANKFUL OLD MAN

Two old men, who had been friends in early youth, met after an interval of many years. A cordial greeting ensued, and then one of them asked the other: "How old are you now?" He said: "Thank God, I am in good health." "Are you well-off in worldly goods?" "Thank God, I am in debt to no man." "Have you any special trouble of mind?" "Thank God, I have no young children." "Have you any enemies?" "Thank God, I have no near relations."

THE THREE SORTS OF HAPPY MEN

In two verses of poetry, Al-Mutanabbi, one of the greatest Arabian poets and philosophers, reduces the number of happy men to three classes. They have been paraphrased and put into English verse by a friend, as follows:

To three life seems a summer sky:
The first who has no mind to know
The heights and depths of life below,
Nor ever asks the reason why.

The second he to whom life's sum
Is self at ease; who never lets
The past disturb with dark regrets,
Nor hopes and fears from days to come.

The third who, led by fancies crude,
In scorn of truth, deceived at heart,
Makes fruitless dreams his better part,
And hollow hopes the highest good.

CYNICAL VIEWS OF LIFE

Abu'l-Ala was another great poet-philosopher. He lost his sight from small-pox early in life, was a cynic and pessimist, and may have often been copied by Omar Khayyam. He refers to his affliction and to the fact that he lived and died an unmarried man (so as to have no children) in a well-known verse:

"Here am I—wronged by my father
Who gave me birth—while I have done wrong to no one."

Some of his poetry has been put into English quatrains by Ameen F. Rihany, in imitation of Omar Khayyam's *Rubaiyat*, and the following, from the *Quatrains of Abu'l-Ala*, are a few striking examples:

"What boots it, in my creed, that man should moan
In Sorrow's Night, or sing in Pleasure's Dawn?
In vain the doves all coo on yonder branch,
In vain one sings or sobs: lo! he is gone.

So solemnly the Funeral passes by!
The march of Triumph, under this same sky.

60

Trails in its course—both vanish into Night:
To me are one, the Sob, the Joyous Cry.

Many a grave embraces friend and foe,
And grins in scorn at this most sorry show;
A multitude of corses passed therein—
Alas! Time almost reaps e'er he doth sow!

How oft around the Well my Soul would grope
Athirst; but lo! my Pail was without Rope:
I cried for Water, and the deep, dark Well
Echoed my wailing cry, but not my hope.

The door of What-May-Be none can unlock,
But we can knock and guess, and guess and knock:
Night sets her glittering sail, and glides along,
Ship-like; but where, O Night-ship, is thy dock?

Oh, when will Fate come forth with his decree,
That I might clasp the cool clay, and be free?
My Soul and Body, wedded for a while,
Are sick, and would that separation be.

If miracles were wrought in bygone years,
Why not to-day, why not to-day, O seers?
This Leprous Age most needs a healing hand,
Oh, why not heed his cries, and dry his tears?"

MISCELLANEOUS PROVERBS

He who treats you as he treats himself does you no injustice.

He who lives on expectations dies in poverty.

Three things are no disgrace to man—to serve his guest, to serve his horse, and to serve in his own house.

Extremes are a mistake—a middle course is the best.

When the cooks are many the food is spoiled. When a ship has two captains it will sink.

Tie the ass where his owner wants.

Be a slave to truth—the slave to truth is a freeman.

No bravery in war can withstand overwhelming numbers.

If God gives you, give you to others.

A horseman has ever an open grave before him.

Confide not in a friend until you have tried him, and fight no enemy until you have sufficient power.

A prudent man is right though he perisheth, and a reckless man is wrong though he cometh out safely.

Trust not in present prosperity, for it is a departing guest.

Reserve the white coin for the black day.

If it be in your power to do harm to your enemy—do it not, but forgive him and win his thanks.

The eye cannot contend with pointed steel.

Be cautious even where you are most sure.

Poverty is a chain which restrains men from doing much evil.

If you would know what a man hath, look not to what he gains but to what he spends.

Nothing can be concealed except that which is not.

The best friend is he who changeth not with the changes of time.

Every rule has exceptions.

The most unjust man to himself is he who humbles himself to one who hates him, and he who praises one whom he does not know.

When you do a kindness, make a small thing of it, though it be a great; and when you receive a kindness, make much of it, though it be small.

Idle hands are unclean.

This world is honey mixed with poison—a joy inseparable from sorrow.

If you are ignorant, inquire; if you stray, return; if you do wrong, repent; and if you are angry, restrain yourself.

Made in the USA
Middletown, DE
27 September 2021